Sherlock Holmes
And
The Case of the Yuletide Puzzle

From recovered manuscripts

of John H. Watson

By

Ed Trotta

First edition published in 1990
© Copyright 2022
Ed Trotta

The right of Ed Trotta to be identified as the author of this work has been asserted by him in accordance with the Copyright, Designs and Patents Act 1998.

All rights reserved. No reproduction, copy or transmission of this publication may be made without express prior written permission. No paragraph of this publication may be reproduced, copied or transmitted except with express prior written permission or in accordance with the provisions of the Copyright Act 1956 (as amended). Any person who commits any unauthorised act in relation to this publication may be liable to criminal prosecution and civil claims for damage.

All characters appearing in this work are fictitious. Any resemblance to real persons, living or dead, is purely coincidental. The opinions expressed herein are those of the author and not of MX Publishing.

Paperback ISBN 978-1-80424-020-5
ePub ISBN 978-1-80424-021-2
PDF ISBN 978-1-80424-022-9

Published by MX Publishing
335 Princess Park Manor, Royal Drive,
London, N11 3GX
www.mxpublishing.com

Cover image by Kathryn Donatelli and

cover design by Brian Belanger

for

Spencer

my daughter

My sincerest gratitude to R. Bruce Connelly for his encouragement in writing this book in the first place. My deepest thanks to Margaret and Markku Tuomi for too many insights to mention. And to Brunonia Barry my heartfelt appreciation for her support throughout my career.

Contents

Foreword		6
Chapter 1	Gifts Exchanged	9
Chapter 2	The Puzzle	18
Chapter 3	Christmas Day	29
Chapter 4	Watson's Business	35
Chapter 5	A Break in the Case	47
Chapter 6	The Visitor	56
About The Author		73

Ed Trotta as Sherlock Holmes

Foreword

The story you are about to read was written over three decades ago, and first came to light when I adapted it for the stage twenty years later. *"Sherlock Holmes and The Case of the Yuletide Puzzle"* had its world premiere at the Summit Theatre in Bluefield, West Virginia in 2008. It was well received, and viewers of the play had great fun trying to beat Sherlock Holmes to the solution of the puzzle. Now, another decade later, it has found its way back into print, suggesting that an enduring Sherlock Holmes story can take some time to reach its entire, destined audience.

Portraying Sherlock Holmes on stage was the inspiration to write for a character I'd come to know from a unique perspective.

I am confident you will find the Yuletide Puzzle as taxing and captivating as its theater going viewers.

Ed Trotta, March 2022

Chapter 1

Gifts Exchanged

"See here, Holmes, it's begun to snow!" I called to my friend from the window of our shared residence at 221B Baker Street.

"Excellent observation, Doctor," Holmes replied drily, "both accurate and succinct."

"Come, Holmes, take a look at it."

"I hardly need to 'look at it,' Watson, unless of course you detect something unique regarding this particular incidence of precipitation. Otherwise, I shall rely entirely upon your report of it to me."

My companion would not deign to so much as look up from his present activity of scanning the week's accumulated dailies for specific articles of interest in order that they might be clipped, and saved, in the endless files which the famous detective had developed as a unique reference library of criminal enterprise.

"Very well, then," I replied, "I shall render an account if that is your petition. This variety of snow, and I should say it registers within the range of what's referred to as a 'flurry' is, um, white…the flakes are large, quite moist, and I suggest that there will be very little accumulation, if at all."

"Mm," my companion responded distantly. Then, "Did you know, Watson, that the bludgeon is still the most popular of all murder weapons? Surprising, in this day of considerable improvements to the reliability, accuracy, and portability of firearms. Doubtless it is the lack of a report to which the cudgel owes its position in this statistic. I don't imagine the unnecessary calling of attention to oneself to be the mark of any self-respecting murderer…"

"Self- respecting… ?!"

"Law enforcement will rue the day when the inconvenience of a revolver's thunderous crack is remedied by some muffling or silencing device. That day will come, old chap…and soon. Mark my words."

"I'd rather not, if it's all the same to you".

"But the bludgeon! Such a brutal means of execution! I should think a large, well-balanced knife would be the preference. After all, if used to sever the larynx it would silence the victim as effectively as..."

"Holmes! Stop, I beg you!" I shouted with such helpless frustration that I finally drew his attention. As he looked up to see me charging at him from my window seat, his expression was one of bewilderment, a rare look indeed on the face of Sherlock Holmes. Still, I would not be placated by this appearance of innocence, whether a facade or genuine. "I am making every effort to enjoy the warmth of this fire, the digestion of Mrs. Hudson's expertly prepared goose, and the perfectly delightful vision of a snowfall on Christmas Eve! It's Christmas Eve, Holmes, and you sit there speculating on and on about bludgeons and knives, severing the larynx, silencing a victim! It's positively intolerable! I should have known better than to try to improve your spirits! I'm familiar with the black mood which comes over you during this holiday, and I wanted...well, instead I find myself hard-pressed to retain my own sentiment of 'good will toward men' with all your talk of how best to murder them! And I'm afraid there's simply too short a supply of good cheer left in me to go 'round." Fuelled, now, by a determination to salvage what was left of my waning gaiety, I found myself in hat and coat at the door to the landing. "I'll just take my leave and let you to your bloody files..." I stopped short in departure and turned to address Holmes. His countenance had altered radically from the dazed expression he'd worn as I had begun my tirade, to one of humility mingled with despair.

"Forgive me, my dear fellow. I'm afraid I shall never master this gift you have of being able to appreciate some sense of spirituality and generosity associated with this season. My view of it all is hopelessly jaded. I consider the snowfall useful to insulation on the window sill, and as a provider of exceptionally clear tracks. That is all. Christmas itself has become little more to me than a crass, commercial excuse which shopkeepers and barmaids embrace to their fullest advantage."

"Barmaids! A capital idea, Holmes! Let's indulge..."

"I was, in my own manner, attempting to contribute to a seasonal atmosphere by refraining from my usual diversion of artificial stimulants. Trust me, Watson, it's an effort." As Holmes gestured toward the Moroccan leather case atop the mantle, I realized that I had been too hard on the poor fellow.

"Let us raise a sherry to Mrs. Hudson's goose," I endeavoured to capitalize on my friend's change of heart. "If you will brave the weather so far as the corner pub, I shall procure a round for everyone in the establishment. We'll toast the old gal's bird with proper merriment amongst our neighbors. Come, Holmes, let's away."

"Out?" he asked. "In this muck?"

"Muck? Oh, Holmes, you are hopeless!"

"I have another idea, Watson. Since only you and I can truly acknowledge the incomparable skill of Mrs. Hudson's cooking, and since I prefer my own stock of sherry to what we're likely to discover elsewhere, I suggest we remain here for our toast. Afterwards, if you're of a mind to hear it, I have a new prelude to perform which I consider absolutely joyous. I presume you'll find it tolerably uplifting. Then," he concluded, "we shall exchange our gifts."

"Gifts?" I was completely taken by surprise.

"Yes, gifts! The new lens which...." my friend froze mid-sentence, having just revealed the item I'd purchased for him on the way to our rooms this very day.

We stood there for a moment of suspension. Every single Christmas since we'd met, Holmes managed to divine what gift I'd picked out for him, and every Christmas he'd found a way to supply me with an item of immeasurable usefulness which I, myself, had not realized

I was lacking. In fact, I must further confess that such was the extent of his self-proclaimed disdain of the occasion, I was more often than not astonished to learn he'd obtained anything for me at all, even though this had never been the case.

Now I was afforded the vision of Sherlock Holmes at a loss for words a second time in one night, while we both, I imagined, contemplated years past in the mutual twinkling of a Christmas Eve. It was this double bedazzlement which remains singular to our Christmas of '89. We broke, simultaneously, into a hearty laugh, shaking hands and slapping each other on the back.

Even as compared to the best of the times I shared with Holmes, I would still proclaim this night as outstanding. His musical virtuosity soared after having toasted every limb, wing, and breast of Mrs. Hudson's goose. Then, upon dismissing his violin to its hard-shell case, Holmes returned to the room with a small, silver box adorned with a card reading simply "John."

"You never cease to amaze me, Holmes," I said as he offered me my gift. "Sometimes I suspect that aversion to sentiment of yours to be nothing more than a ruse to conceal your truer nature." A shadow of confusion seemed to pass over my companion at this, and so I hastened to change the subject. "I suppose it hardly makes sense for me to go through the trouble of wrapping my gift to you. You always know what it is," I laughed as I strode to the rack to extract his gift from my coat pocket. "I ask this every year, but how *did* you know ... "

"Such knowledge is a simple matter when the suggestion is made in advance," he interrupted. "You were the one going on about your infernal Christmas shopping last week when we passed Bickerson's Exchange where I first spotted this wonderful specimen of a lens. Knowing this to be your preoccupation at the moment, I had then but to be certain that my admiration of the item was subtle enough to appear spontaneous, yet obvious enough to receive your notice. I have made requests of you before by such means, Watson, and you've never disappointed me," he continued as he accepted the package. "It has a nice weight to it, doesn't it, Watson?" he beamed. "I knew it would. The latest techniques in the manufacture and grinding of glass promise to provide an absolute exactness of composite density, all of which contribute to the elimination of those troublesome arcs of color that appear with the use of lenses possessing a less precisely consistent, refractive property."

By now, he had opened the box and proudly held aloft the great magnifying glass by its handsome, ebony handle. Holmes' eyes sparkled with unmitigated joy as he brandished the lens over every object within reach.

"Magnificent, Watson! Remarkable! Oh, this is absolutely first-rate! What unparalleled clarity! Oh, my dear fellow, I cannot thank you enough! There is no distortion, no hellish rainbows about everything! Thank you!"

"You are quite welcome, Holmes." My disappointment that I was unable to surprise my companion again this year was replaced by the satisfaction of seeing his unbridled pleasure.

"And what have we here?" I asked, returning our attention to my gift as I opened it anxiously. It was a pen, one such as I had never seen before. The stout barrel was of a dark, pearl texture adorned by three gold bands about the center, matched by a gold clip and nib.

"Oh, Holmes, this is quite a handsome instrument!" I exclaimed.

"Befitting my biographer," he added. "It has a singularly large reservoir cavity for the ink. I reasoned that I shall probably never succeed in my efforts to persuade you to write *less*, and so I decided to facilitate your customary embellishments of our adventures with this gift. Here, use my glass to examine the monogram on the clip."

"Thank you, Holmes, and Merry Christmas."

At that moment, there arose the sound of voices lifted in song from the foot path below. I hastened to the window and discovered a handful of carolers engaged in a rousing version of "Deck the Halls". It was a delightful vision, these singers huddled together against the cold, in their colorful attire, while the snow continued to fall and swirl about them. I immediately searched my pockets for whatever coins I could find and swept my desktop for an additional few. Holmes declined to join me at the window, preferring to remain in his wingback chair.

I waited for a pause in the music to toss the first few coins at the carolers' feet. Presently, they resumed the entertainment with "Silent Night", during which I gradually dispensed additional change down to them. At a point, Holmes erupted.

"Another shilling, Watson, and you will have wasted sufficient funds to afford a seat at the theatre for some proper amusement."

"Wasted?"

"On a cluster of our neighbors offering their rendition of a few Christmas ditties.

"Humph...'ditties'? And how do you know how much I've given them in return?"

"I'll do better than explain, Watson. I shall now demonstrate". With that, Holmes produced a coin from his own pocket and immediately hurled it against the stone of the hearth. It struck and bounced out of sight. "Now then, what denomination was that currency?"

"Well, I can't be certain of course, but it sounded like... it sounded like? Oh Holmes, don't tell me you deduced the amount I spent by calculating the values of the coins according to the sound they produced as they struck the stone!"

"As you wish, Watson. I need not 'tell you' as you've just deduced my method. Congratulations."

"That's impossible, Holmes, simply impossible".

"Not to a musically accomplished ear, Watson. The tones produced can be likened to notes on a scale. I will admit that I was forced to estimate on a minor level, owing to the similarity of the crown to the double florin. Being essentially identical in weight, I chose to evaluate the average of the resonance produced by those particular coins."

"You were able to add the values that quickly and produce a sum?!" I was understandably stupefied by such a feat.

"Yes, old fellow, such rapid addition was indeed more challenging than identifying each coin's worth."

I took a seat and mused on this hitherto unknown talent my companion possessed. A half hour later, I was still wondering how this skill could be employed to assist in the process of a consulting detective's work. The carolers had since dispersed, and a sudden tolling of the clock tower broke the ensuing silence.

"Well, Holmes, it is now officially Christmas" I offered in as cheery a manner as I could summon.

"Quite so", he replied, "and therefore proper that I return your earlier well wishes by bidding you a very… happy holiday indeed."

"Thank you, Holmes, and again, Merry Christmas".

Chapter 2

The Puzzle

"Here comes Mrs. Hudson," exclaimed Holmes with some surprise as we heard her familiar tread on the stairs. Holmes and I had just exchanged Christmas greetings without noticing the pertinence of the timing, for as Mrs. Hudson knocked, the church bells were still tolling while the clock tower heralded midnight.

"A delivery, Mr. Holmes," our landlady announced through the door. Holmes' eyes flew open wide as he elevated straight up and out of his chair, bolting to the window overlooking the entrance to 221B Baker Street. He swung open a half and leaned so far out over the sill I thought he would be gone by the time I could raise myself to follow him.

"The door, Watson!" Holmes called urgently. I hesitated but a moment and he added, "Mrs. Hudson!" but suddenly he was already inside again and passing me on my way to admit the woman. He threw open the door, simultaneously reaching for something he knew would be there. "Thank you, Mrs. Hudson," my friend said, as he snatched the single envelope from her tray. Then he turned from the proprietress to examine the item at arm's length, holding it steadily to the light. I felt an impulse to afford the poor woman some further acknowledgement.

"My compliments on the preparation of our Christmas goose, Mrs. Hudson. Holmes and I have just now finished toasting to it...or rather, to your...er..."

"Yes, it was exquisite," Holmes came to my rescue. "My sincerest apologies for this disturbance at so late an hour. A very urgent matter, I assure you." With that, he closed the door in the landlady's face.

"And Merry Christmas," I added through the closed door. "Really, my good man," I began a half-hearted admonishment of what I considered unseemly behavior on the part of my companion. "You really ought not take advantage of her that way. After all…."

"Delivery indeed!" Holmes interrupted, "On Christmas eve, at the precise stroke of midnight?"

"Quite right, Holmes," I had to admit that the timing was so exact as to doubt it could be attributed to coincidence. "Still," I ventured, "why this sudden urgency? Why assume the worst? It could be that some utterly harmless, well-wishing acquaintance…"

"I *assume* nothing, Watson, least of all the worst. This is a concept you seem to have a difficulty mastering. What you call urgency, I consider fervour. As for any well-wishing acquaintances, even had I not eliminated that possibility by accounting for every one of them in the instant that Mrs. Hudson announced the arrival of this dispatch, I would now be able to do so as a result of my initial inspection of the stationery."

"What does it tell you, Holmes?"

"A moment, Watson. My new lens, would you be so good?"

"Of course, Holmes," I was enormously gratified that the glass which I had just presented to my companion, within that very hour, was now being summoned to its first assignment on a matter of some apparent import.

"Yes, thank you, Watson," Holmes burned with excitement as he took the instrument from me and brought it to bear on the envelope, still sealed, which he held delicately in his other hand. "Now we shall inspect this impertinent article with significantly more authority than has ever been at my disposal, thanks to you."

"Thanks to my gullibility," I corrected my friend, as I was indisposed to claim more than any reasonable apportionment of credit in the selection of the magnifying lens as a suitable Christmas gift for my colleague. "I was little more than an executor of your considerable will."

"Nonsense," Holmes replied distractedly as he continued his analysis of the object, "your constant attentiveness to my every interest or concern is responsible for the manifestation of this instrument, much more so than my manipulation of that vigilance."

This line of reasoning could not be refuted, and I realized that my fondness for the man, as evidenced by his management of it, was the true nature of my bequest. After all, I concluded, who else could possibly endure him?

"Just as I feared," Holmes' proclamation curtailed my reflections.

"What?" I asked anxiously, for his tone implied a profound anxiety. "What is it?"

"Nothing," he responded, as gravely as I had ever heard him speak. "Nothing at all. Never have I perceived an object so absolutely devoid of clues as this insidious item," he said, shaking it vigorously in his grip. "And," he added, waving the lens in his other hand, "viewed it with such an alarming *proximity*!"

"Then the magnifying glass could not..."

"The glass is but an increasement factor, Watson. It is a mathematical constant that naught multiplied by any power, remains naught. There is no fault with the lens. The paper of which this packet is composed happens to be among the most common products of England. It is a crude pulp, somewhat translucent, with a finish resistant to moisture. It's commonly utilized to wrap meat, fish, poultry, and any other number of consumable goods at the time of purchase. Its use is prevalent among butchers and merchants in virtually every sector of the country. Further, observe how this clasp was designed." Here, Holmes thrust the object of our scrutiny toward me, so that I instinctively reached to take it into my own possession. He deftly jerked it away, however, with a cautioning look, as he carried on. "Notice how cleverly the need for any adhesive is avoided in the construction. Doubtless, you have already concluded that the envelope is of a self-made variety, owing to my description of the paper."

"Mm, doubtless," I interjected.

"It is an ingenious creation, how the outer flap is designed to tuck neatly into the convergence of the other three edges, and so hold them in place. Of course, there are no watermarks, no prints or smudges, and no post-mark as the thing was hand delivered."

"It was hand-delivered!" I repeated, for I felt sure that this fact would avail the detective of an entirely other avenue of investigation. "Perhaps we should question Mrs. Hudson as to who it was brought her the message in the first place."

"I know who it was, or very nearly," Holmes smiled ruefully. "You recall how my instinct led me to the window overlooking the entrance upon Mrs. Hudson's appearance?"

"Led you?" I asked incredulously, "it fairly pushed you out!"

"Quite so," Holmes replied. "I was endeavouring to maintain my view of the messenger for as long as possible."

"Did you see him then?"

"Yes, though I fail to grasp how you deduced that the bearer of this delivery was masculine. Nevertheless," Holmes forged on, having effectively and efficiently reminded me of this recurring lesson, "this item was put into Mrs. Hudson's hand by a lad of approximately twelve to fourteen years, a street urchin I should judge by his ragged attire. I was afforded but a second or two of his appearance as he rounded the corner so swiftly that I have not the slightest doubt he was chosen to take part in this episode for that very ability."

"But surely we could track him down, Holmes," I pleaded. "The trail is fresh, and you said yourself that snow is a provider of excellent traces. We'll round up Toby..."

"We'll do no such thing," Holmes countered. "There is every reason to believe we might enjoy success in the effort you propose of locating this individual, though I promise you such an undertaking would be abundantly more demanding than you estimate. Our young accomplice probably wears shoes worn smooth of any tread which bear little relationship to the actual size of his feet, for one thing. But more, the juvenile street life of London live nowhere and everywhere, with rarely so much as a name to distinguish them from each other. There is no pattern to the routine of their daily existence, and they dissolve into the mass of humanity like salt into boiling water. In short, Watson, the very qualities which we find admirable in the Irregulars, when they are employed on our behalf, render them practically invulnerable to exposure when they wish to be invisible. No, Watson, we'll not expend our energies in pursuit of the intermediary. I will advance our inquiry regarding the boy to the Irregulars themselves. Perhaps something will come of it, but I doubt he would be of much use to us in any event. There is but one recourse left us," Holmes concluded.

"Which is?"

"We shall now *open* the letter, my good fellow."

I knew that it was Holmes' method to extract every available shred of data from each phase of an investigation before proceeding to the next, but I was confounded by the realization that we had yet to disclose the contents of the note!

"Wouldn't that be cheating, Holmes?" I asked, as my companion set the article down and began to carefully unfold the intersection of the crimped edges. "Don't you want to deduce what it says *before* you look at it?" I knew I'd gone too far with this last remark, for my friend directed an uncustomary, side-long glance at me, even in the midst of his delicate work.

"More than you suspect, Doctor," he quipped. "Ironic, that your tepid mockery should be among the more astute of your observations. You really ought to allow it more often."

"Oh, rubbish!" I returned, "You're obviously determined to ferret out a perplexity where none exists, owing to your recent inactivity. You've nothing there but a Christmas greeting from someone you've overlooked. Yes," I dared repeat it, "overlooked! After all, we've no proof… "

Were I able to retrieve these words before they had reached my companion's ears, I would have surrendered a month's wages to do so, for as I spoke, the envelope yielded its final crease and thence unfolded of its own accord, like a hand with unfurling fingers, to proffer the object shrouded within its grasp.

"Proof, Doctor?" Holmes' question hung heavily about us for what seemed an eternity of dark imaginings. The aging fire was the only sound as it crackled and spit, sending shivering swells of crimson throughout the room.

What held my companion and I so mesmerized in its spell was a twice folded, single sheet of paper, the same material as its encasement which, when Holmes smoothed it flat, revealed that it was covered with markings of the strangest variety I had ever seen.

The single page measured nine inches square. Holmes counted one hundred eighteen impressions upon it, which were spaced so as to effectively cover the surface. The markings themselves were made with a black ink which Holmes identified as the most common variety to the city's stationers, and so untraceable in every regard. The array of imprints including streaks, dots, curves, and lines, gave the impression of an Eastern language when viewed at a glance; perhaps Hindi, Kurdish, or even Sanskrit. Our combined knowledge of tongues, however, was sufficient to suggest that such was not the case. Subsequent investigation, conducted extensively by Holmes, would reveal that no established vocabulary or dialect was inherent in the cryptogram.

"What do you make of it, Watson?"

"I can't make anything of it, Holmes," as indeed I could not, and the quantity of sherry I had consumed was beginning to render me incapable of making much sense, or use, of anything. "And you?" I asked, for the nature of this curious dispatch befitted my companion's particular talents as a specific key is suited to its own lock.

"Hm," Holmes responded. "My lens again, if you please."

As I offered the instrument to my friend for a second, or should I say third, time, I observed the force with which the cypher drew him in. Even as the single page, in all its mystic significance, repelled me, the power it exacted on Holmes was doubly magnetic.

In fact, the only element more profound than Holmes' preoccupation with the puzzle was my own sudden weariness. The evening's revelry had taken its toll upon my senses.

"Well," I began, "it's plain I'm of no further use here...suppose I'll take my leave...Holmes."

"Mm," my friend replied, as though a million miles from the heart of London.

"Yes...well, to bed then. Good luck with the cypher," I added, realizing, too late, the error of this utterance.

"If *luck* becomes a factor, Watson," Holmes retorted, "I'll summon you."

I had not the energy to confront him on the issue of well wishes summarily reduced to inaccurate statements, and so I made my way to my own quarters without risking another word. As I prepared for bed, the rattle of the iron hearth-grate as Holmes doubtless stoked and revived the blaze, foretold of the endless night which beckoned to my companion. I envied him this interval of passionate involvement, as I had known such on occasions of my own professional concerns. I was, nevertheless, thankful not to *be* Sherlock Holmes, for I could never endure the dependencies with which he was afflicted, and my situation as his companion afforded me every delight of his adventuresome career without the burden of its realities. As I closed my eyes this early Christmas morning, my imagination prevailed upon me a visage of my friend, the famous detective, as he drew from the embers a remnant taper to set it, smoldering, atop the tobacco packed into his favorite pipe.

Cypher Image #1

Chapter 3

Christmas Day

I slept in Christmas morning, as was my constitution's preference in response to the celebration of the previous night. Upon awakening, my pocket watch revealed the hour to be close on noon, indicating an indulgence of sleep which I further attributed to the quiescence of a London holiday, enhanced by a thick, muffling blanket of snow. I reflected on my own observation the previous night that there would be little, if any, accumulation. I quit my room to discover Holmes of a disposition which confirmed my imagining of his nocturnal vigilance. He had spent the night in a reconstruction of the cypher on a scale that enabled it to be studied from his wingback chair while it hung fixed to an easel which Holmes kept for just such occasions as this. I left him to his devices amid the stench of stale tobacco smoke and accumulative hearth ash, to afford myself a proper atmosphere in which to dine. Afterwards, I took a turn by Anderson's apothecary. Finding it closed for repairs as well as the Christmas occasion, I returned to Baker Street by foot. It had been, upon reflection, an altogether uneventful Christmas day.

Upon entering our rooms, I observed that my companion took no notice of my arrival. His posture did not alter in the least as he sat in contemplation of his latest case. Perhaps I should say his latest mystery, for the elusive cryptogram had yet to yield its secret to my friend, and it remained a solitary puzzlement which had been thrust upon us by an unseen hand close on twenty-four hours hence.

Until the code was broken and the mystery divulged, it could not be certain whether or not an investigation would ensue. Still, it was difficult to imagine that anything so diabolically created would have been done so for its own sake. Such was my companion's devotion to the puzzle that I was startled to hear him address me so casually.

"Take heart, my good fellow, the apothecary promises to reopen tomorrow noon, and you shall be availed of your liniment as well as some relief from your present discomfort."

"It's my own fault, Holmes," I replied. "Imagine, me a doctor and not having the good sense to supply myself of...wait a minute, Holmes! I walked up those stairs being particularly cautious not to favour my injury which this blasted cold snap is antagonizing beyond tolerance. And it was for your sake I did so! I know how involved you've become with this cryptogram business, and I wished not to distract you with concerns for my condition. I am well aware that the inflammation produced in my shoulder has its way of affecting my stride. Furthermore, I made my way directly to the fire, delighted that you'd seen fit to have one roaring, and so I fail to see…"

"How could you 'fail to see' when you've just succinctly described several of my most elucidating clues? Forgive me for chastising you on this one, Watson. I really am most appreciative of your efforts to conceal what you consider a 'distraction' from my work, but I am disappointed that you could not follow the logic I employed to arrive at my conclusion. You said yourself that you were particularly cautious to not favour your wound in your ascent of the hall stairs. Quite so! In fact, you were overly protective of my concentration, and so your gait bore even less of its usual pronouncement of cadence than is typical for you. Also, by your own observation, you made your way directly to the fire. This is not your custom, Watson, and how often have I said that there is a reason, whether broad or minute, for every divergence from habit? You invariably enter these premises and divest yourself of hat, cloak, and medical bag before settling in front of the hearth, sometimes going so far as to supply yourself with a cup of tea before doing so. Your current behavior is as far from this as the Orient from Trafalgar Square! Really, Doctor, I am more than disappointed. I am insulted! I have honed the many and varied skills of my deductive powers to a point which I depend upon to pierce the armor of a stranger's conscious facade, and now my constant companion, my biographer, indeed, my only friend presumes to *fool* me?! And to what ends? To avoid being a distraction? Well, ironically it may amuse you to learn that the observations of which we speak regarding the effect of this inclement weather on your Afghan keepsake, coupled with this notice," here Holmes fairly flung the daily report at me, "that the pharmaceutical establishment, which you favour for its location convenient to passage home, 'would be closed to the public for reconstruction of the storefront'...these observations were not difficult! They were made with an absolute minimum of effort and required substantially less energy of me than I am expending at this very moment!"

Here, Sherlock Holmes collapsed back into his velvet, wingback chair and brought his attention to bear, once again, on the cryptogram fixed to the easel across the room. Then, with a wave of disgust and surrender, Holmes turned from both the cryptogram and me to compose himself with two fingers pressed against either side of his temple. For my part, I reasoned that it would behoove me to endure the awkwardness of the moment without a word, for I knew my friend's volatility to be equalled by his sense of fairness. I depended upon him, at such times as these, to acquit me of any guilt without the necessity of a defense.

"Forgive me, Watson," Holmes finally broke the dreadful silence which followed his outburst. "My patience is threadbare. Worse, it is less than non-existent, it has become a negative factor. Unfortunately, you've just undeservedly borne the weight of my frustration. I ought to be indebted to you for the diversion, however brief, whether intended or not." Now the famous detective lowered his hand from his head and turned toward me with a benign expression. It seemed to be the first time he looked at me since our exchange of gifts the preceding night.

"Even had your little charade been successful," he continued gently, "I should now reach the same conclusion by observing your position by the hearth and the way you've managed to favour yourself towards the heat. By the way, Watson, the fire is not a coincidence. I am pleased to hear that you took delight in finding it lit. It was for your sake that I asked Mrs. Hudson to light it. You see, Doctor, not only was I aware of your condition as you entered. I anticipated it. I prefer to avail myself of the dailies first thing in the morning, upon their arrival, while you are content to peruse them at your leisure later in the day. It is no mystery, therefore, that I was privy to this particular notice of the apothecary being reopened on the morrow, while you were not. This fact, coupled with the distinct scent of vinegar which permeated these premises last night, the same aroma which accompanies your every usage of that facsimile of a liniment you've concocted on more than one occasion, was sufficient information for me to predict your desire for some natural warmth upon your return today."

"How absolutely ironic, Holmes," I fairly chuckled, for I was touched by my companion's thoughtfulness even more than I was impressed by his deduction, "We've had this little riff as a result of our both concerning ourselves with each other's best interests."

"Exactly, Watson. Let us remember this incident, for it serves as an excellent example of how one's own concerns are the only ones worthy of administration. What is the American expression? We should 'mind our own business,' yes?"

I did not agree that this had been the instruction put forth by my friend's conclusion, but I declined to say so, preferring to leave well enough alone by replying simply, "Yes, Holmes, that's the expression."

Chapter 4

Watson's Business

True to Holmes' word, and the *Chronicle's* announcement, Anderson and Sons resumed dispensation of their pharmaceuticals the following noon, and I embraced the opportunity to properly attend my aching clavicle. Either motivated by my own advice that exercise is the best remedy of such afflictions as I now tolerated, or a conscious rehearsal of the manner in which I now anticipated performing my ascent of the hall stairs on Baker Street, I found myself delaying my return in favour of making unscheduled visits 'round to the residences of a few, newly acquired patients who, I suspected, would be receptive and perhaps grateful for the additional attention. This proved a worthwhile course, for when I finally did arrive at my shared lodgings, I was so preoccupied with the ills of others, both profound and incidental, that I completely forgot to calculate how much, or little, to falter on the stairs. This, I realized as I faced the entrance door, having already climbed the long stairway, was the best that I could have hoped for.

"Watson! Where have you been?" exclaimed Holmes before I'd managed to fully enter the room. I was totally gratified by both his enthusiasm to see me and his genuine inquiry which suggested he had no knowledge of my recent whereabouts. To top it all, he made no reference to my gait.

"Well," I said, "if I had known I was expected to render an account of my whereabouts, I certainly would offer one, but I am rather inclined to say 'oh, here and there'."

"Well then, how is young Master Richardson surviving his respiratory ailment? I trust nothing more malignant than a seasonal influenza has befallen the lad?" I stood stock still and held the door handle for balance, so scarcely had I entered the room than my companion seemed to read my very thoughts. "Come, come, my good fellow," Holmes continued in a soothing voice, speaking to me as one speaks to a madman, "surely you did not misinterpret my question, 'Where have you been?' as an inquiry of your whereabouts. It is an expression, Doctor, which I believe classifies as an idiom, designed to convey a curiosity less of where one has been than what has kept one. You see, when the spoken accent is on the verb, to be, 'been'…"

"Yes, Holmes, I see," I managed to blurt in time to excuse myself from the imminent lecture, and resolved to survive this recent assault on my privacy by clinging, with concealed desperation, to my usual habits with as much ease as I could summon. I turned from my companion to hang my bowler and coat on the oak tree by the door, setting down my medical bag to do so, but not forgetting to survey the fur collar and hat brim for any signs which might have contributed to his sinister deduction. Yes, it struck me as altogether evil in its cold, cruel accuracy. I struggled to divine the means by which my friend had drawn so complete a picture of my recent activity.

Then Holmes added, "I am only surprised that you forestalled your visit to young Richardson until the last of the day, as your interest in his case is so acute, though perhaps it is also logical to attribute import to a particular patient by affording him your final and, therefore, most generous attention." My companion said this with genuine innocence, as if requesting my confirmation that such was, in fact, the general consensus among physicians.

The effect upon me, however, was like that of a considerable blow to my unprotected midsection. My breath escaped me, and I found myself grasping the oak tree for support with slightly trembling hands. I realized that I needed to recline for equilibrium, and endeavoured to conceal the halting passage to my chair by way of saying, "Yes, Holmes, it's true that I prefer seeing patients whose cases particularly interest me at the close of my rounds so that I can afford us, both, the luxury of as much time as either requires."

By now, I had managed to discover some minor security by seating myself down into the familiar hollow of my own fire-side chair, raising my feet to drape them across the small ottoman adjacent. I noticed, then, some remains of mud on my shoes. I immediately looked elsewhere to suppress this revelation from Holmes and added, with nonchalance, "You appeared anxious to see me, Holmes. Could it be you've made some progress in this cryptogram affair which you are eager to apprise me of?" I decided to distract my friend from the issue of my recent activities and thereby grant myself the additional reward of offering a deductive hypothesis of my own. Normally, such efforts on my part elicited an amusement from my companion but, on this occasion, it had the opposite effect. Holmes' expression darkened as he now withdrew from me and appeared to sink into an abyss of doubt.

"My progress has been minimal at best," Holmes admitted. "I have applied every known decoding method to this infernal cypher without extracting a message of any sort."

"Well, that's something," I offered. My purpose, at this juncture, was to supply my friend with some sense of achievement, or at least hope. "You might take some satisfaction with having deduced how *not* to approach the solution."

"Yes, I might...were that my goal," Holmes replied quietly, "However, the process of elimination is but a means, Watson, which I employ often in the course of unraveling possible interpretations of countless circumstances. It is not an ends, nor can it ever be construed as such, for the eliminative means of reasoning itself fails to exist until such time as it has been drawn to conclusiveness. No, my good fellow, I'm afraid there exists, for me, an impenetrable distinction between effort and accomplishment."

The sudden despair with which Holmes spoke was alarming to me, for I had known his fits of rage, his unendurable egotism, and the spells of sullen blackness which overcame him with varying degrees of regularity, but I had never witnessed this purgatory. He appeared now upon the brink of surrender which, I feared for Holmes, would be more devastating than his demise. I resolved, therefore, to bolster his spirit by any means I could devise.

"Well, this is a switch," I began, "to see you so utterly baffled. Imagine the laugh Gregson and Lestrade will have at your expense if word gets out that Sherlock Holmes was confounded...for the first time in his career! ...by a simple puzzle!" I awaited the full force of my companion's fury.

"Indeed," to my horror, Holmes concurred with my absurd proposal, "I daresay it won't stop at those two. The whole of Scotland Yard is likely to get in on it."

"Well then," I decided to abandon this fruitless approach, "let's leave it at that. Perhaps it's as well. Now then, would you mind enlightening me as to your deductions regarding my business this day?" Holmes' reply was but a chilling, vacant stare. "You appeared to know as much of my recent affairs as I when I entered a while ago...I suppose the earthen remains on my shoes have had quite a tale to tell...haven't they?... Holmes?"

"Yes," he mused at length, "quite a tale."

"So? What else?" I asked as lightly as possible, "You know from my study in these very rooms that respiratory afflictions happen to be of a particular concern of mine. It's quite a natural assumption that such was the ailment of my most recent patient."

"*Assumption?*" Holmes queried with a particular grotesqueness of sincerity which, in my companion, was a hopeful sign.

"Very well then, Holmes," my voice strained to effect calmness, "have it your way."

"Oh, Watson, please grant me this indulgent invasion which, I realize, is conducted at your expense but by which, I assure you, I intend not the slightest offense. You are my friend, Watson, and the only one with whom I dare to trifle in this way because I am assured, you see, that no matter how deeply I probe into the details of your existence, I shall never be required to ultimately deduce anything more horrible than goodness. You cannot imagine how dependent I've become on that rare security, old fellow. The imagined 'secrets' of others which, to me, are often as obvious as *hats* can be… somewhat disquieting." Sherlock Holmes spoke of this to me with a certain penitence and regret which I found so disarming and genuine that I was ashamed of my failure to fully appreciate the burden of his gift, for vision such as my companion possessed could hardly be considered a boon.

"Holmes", I inquired with genuine concern, "can you not avert your eyes from such evidence? Can't you prevent your deductive reasoning from carrying forth with its observations?"

"No, Watson", my friend confessed with a certain sadness, " it is quite involuntary".

"Well," I offered, "I don't mind being the object of your deductive exercises, so long as I'm recompensed with the process of your findings. On this occasion, I should be enlightened as to those details which eluded me".

"Very well, my good fellow!" replied Holmes with a sense of recovery, "Recompensed you shall be! Now then, I'm not certain where to begin as there are several points you might find... instructive. Suppose we begin with the question of your whereabouts. You should have considered your shoes first in this line of inquiry, not your bowler and cloak which, ironically, became devoid of clues once you'd taken them off. It is difficult, at best, to study one's self, Watson, as the examination is likely to alter evidence. For example, the condition of your overcoat prior to your divesting it; the upturned collar, the excess of moisture about the shoulders and one side only, suggested that you'd taken passage by ferry or launch recently, where one is likely to be unevenly exposed to marine elements. You were quite correct to put forth the determination that the remnants of mud on your shoes had ' quite a tale to tell,' but not enough of one, I'm afraid, to deduce much by them alone. There were two distinct types of mud in evidence. The more obvious variety, which you encountered more recently, and so which obscured your earlier visits--this, by the way, Watson, is how I deduced that your attendance on young Richardson was forestalled until the end of your rounds--at any length," Holmes continued, now barely able to keep up with his own reasoning process, "this more prevalent type of earth is most characteristic among growers of produce such as cabbage and other leafy garden crops. There are many small, subsistence farms of this nature which would have required your coming into contact with the mulch I have just described to you, due to area limitation which precludes any proper walkway or planking. There is only one, however, with which I believe you to be acquainted, requiring passage by ferry.

"Richardson's," I managed to add.

"Precisely," Holmes replied, "We've both known Richardson the elder for a good many years, and it is only recently that I observed the addition of 'Richardson, Esq.' to your medical files. I don't peruse your professional records in your absence, Watson, but you subconsciously make something of a fuss over your newly acquired patients so that their individual dossier is often atop your desk for a full day or two before finding its way into the company of your other patients.

"But I was correct regarding the lad's condition? I mean, how you deduced it?"

"Not exactly, Watson," said Holmes, the light returning to his eyes. "What you proposed, that I should arrive at my conclusion based upon your general interest in respiratory ailments, would indeed have been an *assumption*, and not a 'natural' one at that, which you also suggested. Your fascination with this study provides information to a later detail. It was your medical bag, Doctor, which you failed to notice was not completely shut as you set it down because you were too busy examining your top coat and bowler. What has kept it from closing properly is an appendage of your stethoscope protruding slightly above the lip. Use of this instrument is generally early in the examination of a patient and so it naturally winds up in its proper place. Only on such occasions as it is practically the sole apparatus of investigation would I suspect that it might be discovered on top of everything else in your kit. I will admit to some doubt regarding my conclusion that your diagnosis was of a seasonal influenza and nothing more threatening. I am aware that there has been some recent progress in defining a greater variety of respiratory disorders that had previously been lumped together into one or two categories."

"Yes," I replied, "everything used to be pneumonic or consumptive. We're just discovering subtle differences in cause, symptom, and treatment. It is a considerable breakthrough."

"And so, of current concern to the entire medical profession, which divests your own renewed interest in the subject of any useful inference," Holmes concluded. "Had young Richardson's prognosis been grave, I'll warrant you would have insisted on his admission to hospital rather than another night in this damp December. His father has survived worse winters than this with a bottle of whisky, which can be more effective than the draughty clapboard houses of that area."

"The boy's lungs were clear and Richardson had managed a warm, dry room for his son," I acknowledged.

"That is well," Holmes replied. "I know you did not detour to the hospital on your return by the degree to which the mud on your shoes had crusted, which eliminates your having Richardson in tow. My deduction regarding your diagnosis, therefore, seemed safe."

"Quite right, Holmes," I could only nod. "Quite right."

"Yes, quite right," my companion intoned distantly. Then, with a roar, "Yes! Of course!" He said this as he was swept to his feet and carried to the board upon which the ineffable cryptogram was still pinned. "Watson, do you recall my initial observations regarding this article upon our receipt of it?" I endeavoured to devise a response before realizing the question was rhetorical. "I was struck by the singular absence of clues. Singular? I mean *absolute*, Watson! There was nothing to deduce from the paper, the envelope, indeed the very puzzlement itself is devoid of any markings or peculiarities which might, otherwise, have contributed to the available information. This, in itself, is a disclosure! Why, my good fellow, the use of adhesive was avoided so as not to provide a line of investigation, however obscure! Is this not a unique quality? And have I not said that distinction, of any nature, is revealing?"

"Yes, Holmes. I believe you have," I managed to interject.

"Now consider this, my good fellow. I recently remarked to you that I had been unsuccessful in the application of every *known* means of deciphering a cryptogram. Do you see the correlation between these points?" I assumed my companion would carry forward in response to his own inquiry and was, therefore, caught off-guard by his apparent expectation of a reply.

"Er...no," I could only answer.

"Why, it is simplicity itself!" Holmes bellowed. "Do you imagine that any riddle, placed into our possession with such unrestricted caution and pains, would be susceptible to *conventional* methods of translation? I-think-not!"

"Nor do I, Holmes."

"I am of a renewed energy, Watson, and I am determined to extract the meaning of this dispatch. It shall require my devotion to the task, for I am challenged to discern a means of concealment never before employed. Thank you, by the way, for that little diversion on the matter of young Richardson. It was a refreshing exercise, and precisely what was required."

"What the doctor ordered?" I asked, more to myself than my friend.

"What?" asked Holmes, already becoming absorbed.

"Nothing."

Cypher Image #2

Chapter 5

A Break in the Case

"Ah-ha!" exclaimed Holmes after a full thirty-six hours of rehabilitated interest in the mysterious case of the abstruse cryptogram.

"What have you surmised then?" I asked my friend.

"*Surmised*?" he retorted. "You are being diplomatic with me again." But beyond the taunt I saw, at last, a spark. "You are loathe to ask 'what have you deduced,' for fear the inconclusiveness should betray my power to support my own precepts." Here my friend drew up his breath, and spoke confidingly to me, "You must never fear to challenge me, Watson. I depend upon you to that end." Then, the animation which accompanied his most profound solutions seized him, as he paced and gestured radically, in his agitated state of discovery. "The cryptogram, when deciphered correctly, reveals *not a message*."

"What then?" I asked, "a map of sorts?"

"Nothing of the sort!" he fairly clapped with delight. I waited for him to continue, anxious to know what mystery was soon to be revealed, but it immediately became obvious that my friend intended to take full advantage of my baited curiosity as he waited for my next reply.

"Please, Holmes," I begged him, not wanting to be made the fool through idle conjectures. "I cannot guess what… "

"Nor should you *guess*," Holmes hissed the word contemptuously.

"Very well then!" I barked, but my own agitation at being so summarily reprimanded did not soften my companion's disappointment at my choice of words. To atone, I endeavoured to apply my own deductive reasoning to the problem. "If this intricate cryptogram, which has eluded you these last few days," I added to secure some measure of sympathy, "reveals neither a message, by which I mean some straightforward statement or question, nor a map of any sort, as you've emphatically pointed out, then could it be an individual's identity as disclosed through, perhaps, a name?"

"Excellent, Watson!" Holmes replied enthusiastically. "You see, you have but to resist surrender for one minute and bring to bear a modicum of logic, and already you are rewarded with the knowledge that you have reasoned! Imagine, my good doctor, if a fraction of the populace of London would only exercise the degree of reasoning you've just illustrated this hour, what a finer and more civilized world we should all enjoy to live in."

"Then I am correct?" I asked, hopefully.

"No, my dear fellow, I'm afraid your conclusion was completely off-track." Though he said this quite sympathetically, I could not help notice the triumph in his reaction. "I was not congratulating you for any success in your deduction. I felt, nonetheless, that you ought to be encouraged to employ it at every opportunity… however limited the results."

"Yes, all right Holmes, I suppose you deserve this opportunity to gloat."

"You mean," he said, "that I am entitled because this particular cryptogram 'has eluded me these last few days'?" The content of sarcasm in this last reference was such that I realized my friend had misinterpreted my plea for some latitude in evaluating my own efforts, for an affront, an outright attack, on his own immeasurable deductive powers. I realized also that my curiosity regarding the solution to the mystery of the puzzle had not abated during this tangent discussion, and that Holmes threatened to refuse me his revelation on this issue if all other such related matters were not resolved to his satisfaction. Hence, I acquiesced.

"Yes, Holmes, I mean to say that it was foolish of me to even presume a contribution on a matter of such obvious intricacy and obtuseness. I did not wish to do so, I beg you to remember, but…"

"But not at all, my good fellow," Holmes responded, "your effort was neither foolish nor presumptuous. You reasoned that since neither a place, as would be implied by the discovery of a map or diagram, was contained in the puzzle--nor a thing, shall we say, such as a message might be considered, that the identity of a person was likely to be the secret locked within the heart of this diabolical seduction--if it can be said that anything born of such cold, cruel brilliance warrants possession of something so frivolous as a heart at all."

As he spoke, Holmes was drawn back to the single sheet which had virtually held him captive since Christmas. It was now close on the eve of a new decade, and the power of that solitary page would not diminish. During the days since our receipt of the coded mystery, my anxiety for Holmes' well-being heightened until it was of paramount concern. There were periods in which the absolute magnetism of that insidious communication seemed to falter, and the spell dissolved. Conversation with my friend on several of such occasions, however, suggested to me that his proclamations of the cryptogram being "random and meaningless symbols of no significance" or "a hoax without import whatsoever," were merely unsuccessful efforts to convince himself of such. Even the consummate actor I knew my friend to be could not conceal the detachment from reality which pervaded every note from his favoured Stradivarius as it mourned and swooned with unearthly emotions throughout the nights of a dispassionate London December.

Perhaps his exclamations of disinterest were offered for my benefit, but they were countered by instances of such absolute concentration that I became professionally concerned for the health of Sherlock Holmes. Without my intervention, I feared, he may have disdained, or worse, forgotten to take sustenance. In fact, my only recompense as a physician during these spells was the fact that Holmes was so driven by this current problem that he absolutely dispensed with the artificial stimulation of his morphine or cocaine solutions. The key to his Moroccan leather case atop the mantle had not been turned throughout the investigation. Now, as my friend again appraised the seemingly incomprehensible markings which covered the singular page, his eyes narrowed and scanned, rapidly and repeatedly, over each and every mark, indeed every millimeter of that accursed puzzle, so that I felt him slipping away again, lost in the endless reverie of his own unrelenting scrutiny.

"Holmes!" I cried, "What does it mean?"

"We shall know soon enough, my friend, soon enough."

"But I thought you said you'd solved…"

"I've *solved* nothing! I've merely made progress by discovering a solitary facet of the cryptogram which I am certain provides a key that will lead to the puzzle's unravelling."

"And what is this quality of the thing, Holmes, if you would be so kind as to put me out of my considerable misery?"

"As you are well aware, Watson, my concentration, my scrutiny, has been devoted to the enlarged version of the cryptogram. Having thwarted me thus far, I sought to be certain that I had recreated the cypher with absolute accuracy. I, therefore, retrieved the original from my desk for comparison's sake. Now let me describe the lighting in the room at that moment."

"The lighting?" I asked, perplexed that this could have any bearing whatsoever.

"Yes, Watson, the lighting is critical to my discovery. You see, though it had grown dark, which I had not noticed owing to my being so absorbed in the cypher, I had yet to light the desk lamp."

"Quite understandable"

"Yes, quite. Now then, the hearth fire was illuminating the larger puzzle with the result that it became perceptible through the translucent paper of the original cryptogram. Owing to my distance from the one, and proximity to the other, the markings on the two separate cyphers emerged as very nearly the same size. Then, and this is the remarkable detail, Watson, I saw for a fraction of a second, a mathematical equation."

"By Jove!" I was genuinely surprised by this information. "Then the overlapping of the two…"

"Yes! The *superimposing* of them revealed that integers were buried among the symbols. They were then assembled into brief calculations and concealed by cleverly splitting the equations along the vertical line and depicting the top and bottom halves in separate locations on the sheet. The symbols for mathematical actions such as multiplication, subtraction, and so forth were treated similarly. The one equation I unwittingly unearthed is but primer school arithmetic. Surprising, as this phase in search of a solution offers an ideal opportunity to further complicate the process. Either our mysterious correspondent hasn't the slightest interest in mathematics, or this simplistic phase presents a respite *from*, perhaps even a scorn *of*, the puzzle's truer, abstruse nature."

"But this discovery of superimposition effectively solves the cryptogram!" I offered with enthusiasm.

"Hardly, Watson. There is the business of examining the cryptogram for other equations without the knowledge of how many there are to uncover. An arduous task I assure you, requiring nearly as much investigation as I have thus far rendered. And then there is the final deciphering."

"*Final deciphering*? But you said the equations were rudimentary examples easily solved."

At this, my friend turned slowly toward me and spoke as a conspirator, a creator of the mystery, rather than as the force which refused to be thwarted by it.

"When interpreted correctly, this cryptogram will yield naught but yet *another cypher!*"

The import of this statement descended upon me like an impenetrable fog, slowly enveloping all in such a diffusion of thickening white that I might just as well have been in the center of the blackest void. I had prepared my ears, my mind, my soul for the onslaught of revelation, for the shattering clarity of sudden, unlimited illumination, and I was now dizzy with confusion.

"Another…another?!"

"Indeed. From meaningless marks and symbols to equations yielding numbers, and then onto the task of interpreting the numerical code into letters for a message."

"But perhaps the numbers themselves are the solution; coordinates on a map, the combination to a vault…".

"A map of what, Watson? And where is this vault you speak of?" Holmes suddenly seemed impatient with me for my erstwhile efforts. "Numbers themselves are useless but for what they conceal. Now let me get on with the business of ferreting out the equations."

I stood still, expecting Holmes to proceed with the task as I observed his progress. Noticing this, he turned again toward me and advised…

"This may take some time."

Cypher Image #3

Cypher Image #4

Chapter 6

A Visitor

Will you take some of this stew, Holmes?" I asked. "You look dreadful, if you don't mind my saying."

"Not at all, Watson," Holmes answered. "Of my considerable vices, I list not vanity... of appearance."

"And what of the stew then?" I pressed, for my companion's normally lean physique had grown absolutely gaunt in the course of the week's duress. What little nourishment Holmes supplied himself was done so begrudgingly, and even then, purely for the sake of dispensing with the threat of starvation as an obstacle to his purpose.

So it was with sleep. Though I shall never believe that anything natural to heaven or Earth was capable of diminishing the clarity with which my friend could bring his keen, observative powers to bear, the eyes which were the instruments of that awesome faculty, became wild and restless.

"No... thank you, Watson," Holmes responded.

"It's a positive vexation to me, Holmes," I countered, "to watch your health become prey to your obsession. Please bear in mind that, as a physician, I have sworn an oath requiring me to administer to the temporal necessities of all. You've aged ten years in the past six days, and yet you insist on ignoring my professional judgement and guidance. It's calloused of you, Holmes. Worse, it is sadistic."

"Ah-ha," my friend exclaimed privately as he continued to exert his skills in the deciphering of the accursed cryptogram. "The integers are not...." Here he trailed off, and I knew that my charge had been perceived as a distant grumbling of no import whatsoever. I resorted, therefore, to the only line of reasoning with which I had experienced some marginal degree of success.

"You are aware, I presume, that your *genius* is maintained by an intricate arrangement of vital systems, all of which contribute to furnish your *brain* with the blood, oxygen, and sustenance it requires to function at *maximum capacity*."

"Set the stew down on the sideboard there," Holmes replied. "Perhaps I'll have an opportunity later…" He trailed off again.

"Shall I clear these other dishes which you've managed to successfully neglect?" I insinuated.

"Whatever you think best, Watson," my companion responded automatically.

"What I think best?" I could not control myself. "What I think best is for you… "

"Yes, Watson! Whatever you think best!" Holmes suddenly bellowed at me. "Whatever you bloody think best, so long as I am afforded a moment's peace to…"

"A moment!" I was incredulous, given the experience of the past six days.

"Very well, then!" Holmes roared back. "A week! A month! A year, if I choose! I cannot tolerate these distractions from my work, Doctor! You have determined the priorities for your survival, and I have done so for mine. You require eight hours rest, three meals a day, and a discernable regularity to the balance of your daily routine. I – do - not! I require mental stimulation as my sustenance, triumph in this regard provides my rest, and I insist upon the liberty to pursue these necessities in lieu of any uniformity to daily habit!"

A lengthy silence ensued. Holmes returned to his study of the cryptogram without apology for the tirade, nor was I of the mind that one was forthcoming. I was well acquainted with every argument my companion employed in the course of this recurring debate, and his line of attack on this occasion was one which I recognized could not, logically, be interpreted as damaging to me, for it did not question the accuracy of my observations, but only the appropriateness of my timing. There would be no rebuttal on my part, as to do so would not only compound the problem at hand, but would require my challenging the supposition that every man is entitled to the management of his own life. I, therefore, quit myself to my chair in quest of some non-invasive activity with which to pass the time. I noticed, then, the week's accumulation of newspapers, hastily discarded, which were heaped beside my companion's armchair. Despite his assertions regarding an independence of routine, Holmes was, nevertheless, loathe to surrender the everyday practice of perusing the dailies. Had I confronted him on this apparent contradiction, he unquestionably would have argued that, during an investigation, this activity was performed for the sole purpose of whatever contribution it might yield to the current problem, and held not the slightest interest in terms of diversion or unrelated information.

Having not yet availed myself of the tabloids for this, the last day of the decade, I now reached over and pinched up a section. This action produced a great rustling of dry, wrinkled paper which, either owing to the lengthy silence preceding it, or to the sensitivity of the moment, resounded with significant command. I cannot be certain if I detected an acknowledgement from Holmes in response to the sound, for I, myself, was startled by it sufficiently to cease the action immediately, settle the paper back down as gently as possible, and let loose my hold. I chose, instead, a book, a gift from Holmes as it happens, and carefully cracked it open to my mark.

It was an audibly quiet day, this last of the decade, lavish with familiar, and so innocuous, sounds of London. Children dismissed from their schooling matured into workers released from their toil. The occasional cobblestoned passage of a carriage distracted me from my reading, or it was punctuated by my friend's private exclamations of discoveries, disappointments, and muttered calculations.

I must have napped, perhaps intermittently, for I was startled by the change of light more than once. I recall my curiosity upon discovering that the stew had transformed into cold beef slices with cabbage and radish. I was glad of the exchange, but I could not revive the memory of Mrs. Hudson's visit. Holmes declined to partake of the beef, preferring to envelope himself in a progressively thickening cloud of smoke. For my part, I considered the consumption of one slice of meat, together with but a sampling of the complementary fare, to be prudent, for it was sufficient and allotted the remainder to provisions for the night which lay ahead. For this reason, I was thankful that Mrs. Hudson had been so disposed as to serve, for our New Year's repast, a cold meal.

Eventually, darkness threatened to prevail, and I took it upon myself to administer the hearth. As I kindled the grate, Holmes increased the light from his desk lamp, and I reflected upon the peculiar impression of the night's illumination being, in fact, steadier than the sun's.

"Watson," my friend spoke suddenly, "Watson, have you the inclination to assist me?" There was a sense of suppressed urgency in this proposal, and yet a simplicity with which my companion spoke, as if conversation between us had paused but for a moment. "Your assistance would be of inestimable service."

"What a preposterous question!" I responded involuntarily. "Do you imagine I have confined myself to these premises throughout the day for any other reason?"

My friend smiled, "We are to the point of requiring transcription, old fellow, and I suspect there's not a moment to lose! Once I determined that the markings could be assembled into arithmetic equations, I eliminated those symbols which were clearly no part of an integer. I replicated the puzzle again, in the same size as the original, and began the process of hunting for numerical calculations by resuming the action of superimposition that brought this quality to light in the first place. As the equations emerged, and could thus be eliminated from further use, the process became more manageable with the discovery of each calculation. The solution to each equation is an integer."

"Then the puzzle translates into nothing but numbers!"

"Which must then be transposed into their alphabetic counterpart, hence the cryptogram yielding yet another cypher, as I've already told you. We shall begin by assigning the numbers that represented solutions in a very traditional way in which "A" is one, "B" is two, and so forth. Elementary, but a reasonable place to start. I'm hopeful that we are close on deciphering the cryptogram".

"Congratulations, Holmes!" I said with unmitigated admiration, for I must admit to having entertained some doubts regarding my companion's prospects for success in his recent conundrum. "My new pen is freshly supplied of ink, and I ought to be dependable for a few hundred words." Just as Holmes had pleased me by the enthusiastic use of my gift, the new lens, I sought to similarly gratify him with a show of delight in my new possession.

"That is well," my companion responded, "but I appraise the situation as demanding our interpretation of one dozen letters only. Then Holmes seemed to read my thoughts, "You needn't be so alarmed. Were this cypher of any respectable length, it would have been much easier to resolve. A discernable pattern then emerges through the incidence of repeated symbols, the proportion and occurrence of vowels to consonants, and so on. In fact, Watson, the succinct report, sufficiently shrouded, as was this," he added, tapping the puzzle itself in emphasis, "is the most elusive of all comprehensions. So, it is in life, eh, my dear fellow?" With this, he ushered me to his easel upon which was mounted the cryptic riddle. Surrounding us there was the refuse of my companion's labours, as evidenced by the accumulation of discarded papers.

"I shall dictate to you the numbers as I solve the equations. You will be so kind as to record these integers as they occur in the alphabet". Following these directions, in but a moment this simple procedure yielded, true to Holmes' word, twelve letters;

"IWUOTHEXGIBN".

I could not fathom what, if anything, the twelve-letters could possibly mean. "Does this word, if I may call it that, hold any significance for you?" I asked.

Holmes' eyes narrowed as he concentrated on the enigmatic assembly of letters. In a moment he offered, "I am somewhat encouraged by an article 'the' appearing in the center. If the remaining nine letters could be converted to something meaningful… no, not yet, Watson. Such effort would entail an exhausting use of 'trial and error'", which I knew to be Holmes' least favorite form of deduction. "We are now to the point of reversing the alphabet for another obvious form of concealment so that 'A' represents twenty-six, and 'Z' becomes number one."

My task was, in essence, purely clerical in nature for my part in this stage of decoding the puzzle. As we functioned in this manner, I found myself inexplicably pleased that I was of some use in the process of assisting my celebrated comrade.

I resumed transcribing the numbers as Holmes announced them into a different assembly of letters;

RDFLGSVCTRYM

"Another disappointment, eh Holmes? Another meaningless grouping of letters." But, as I looked to my friend for his response, he was already gone. "Holmes!" I shouted. "Where are you?"

"It is neither a disappointment nor meaningless, Watson!" Holmes called from his bedroom amid the distinct sounds of his rummaging about. "It is phonetical!"

This information warranted my reconsideration of the enigma before me. I reasoned that, if phonetical, I had only to vocalize the qualities of the letters, as associated to each other, to be apprised of their significance. I set about this undertaking eagerly, verbalizing a variety of possible pronunciations.

Holmes interrupted my efforts by calling, "What is the time, Watson, precisely?"

"Four minutes to midnight," I replied, glancing at the mantle clock. My companion responded with an unintelligible stretch of oaths and exclamations amid the continued ransacking of his private chambers.

I returned to my purpose of identifying the significance of the code through a continual utterance of the sounds which they might produce, whereupon Holmes, no doubt wearied of my endeavours, shouted, "RED FLAG'S VICTORY!"

I repeated the phrase, "Red Flag's Victory," with some degree of gratification, for it certainly satisfied the phonetic requirement, yet I remained ignorant of the relevance of this expression.

"Then what of the final 'M' Holmes?" I urged of my companion, as though this letter alone had accounted for my confusion.

"The signature, Watson!" Then, "What is the time?"

"Two minutes of the hour," said I, whereupon I took to considering the importance of this other matter regarding the identity of our obtuse correspondent. 'M,' I concluded, could only indicate the involvement of Moriarty, the archrival of my friend, and so villain to myself and all that I regarded as defendable. I surmised, further, that the object of my companion's quest in his private quarters must necessarily have been some device with which he proposed to apprehend the scoundrel, and that this capture was imminent owing to the constant reference of the precise hour. I, therefore, took it upon myself, in support of this observation, to secure the provision of my service revolver from its constant place in my own bedroom. This activity required but a fraction of a minute to accomplish, as I am of a disposition to be specifically aware of firearms within my possession. It was sufficient time, however, to evoke a curiosity concerning my companion's apparent difficulty in locating such munitions, for I knew him to be of a similar attitude in this regard.

Upon my return to the drawing room, I discovered Holmes precariously balanced without the street front window, not unlike his pose when first this cryptogram had been delivered. In his hands he held an expanse of fabric, coloured red, which he proceeded to affix onto the window sill. Now, as the clock tower began its heraldry of a new year, and the unmistakable sound of a two-wheeler echoed down the corridor of Baker Street, I hastened to my companion's aid, revolver in hand to double the blows intended for the loathsome Moriarty.

Upon discovering my situation beside him, however, Holmes flung me aside with a most determined effort, whereon I found myself sprawled suddenly, and helplessly, across the floor. The element of surprise had been to his advantage, I assure you, for I am not so readily dismissed to that position. As I opened my mouth in protest, another voice curtailed my tongue.

"Ho-ho, Sherlock! Bravo for you, old man! I see you've unravelled my little message!" I was aware that the carriage had drawn to a halt beneath the window, and I was now privy to the following dialogue from my prostrate condition.

"Yes!" replied my friend, "It was quite a little test! I must congratulate you on its invention!"

"A mere diversion, Sherlock!" the other voice responded. "I assure you, I had quite as much sport in the formulation of it as you must have had in the deciphering."

"Then it has served us both well! You'll be pleased to learn that it was all the challenge I required this holiday, such that I managed to resist the lure of my chemical stimulants."

"As I had hoped. Merry Christmas, Sherlock, and thank you for this splendid new top hat."

"You're most welcome. It suits you. Will you come up?"

"I only would have done so to gloat, but you've beaten me with your red flag."

"*Our* red flag," my friend hastened to correct. "I am disappointed you failed to recognize…"

"Very well," the other interjected, "*our* red flag which, since you've ventured to remark upon it, still bears the disposition of something that has been packed away for too many years, if I may say so. As evidenced by the severity of the creases traversing its length and breadth, I should judge you've just now mounted it! I'll wager you a shilling that, in an hour, its own weight, together with the evening's damp, will have it smooth as it was in our youth!"

Thereupon, the clock tower completed its overture in reception of the New Year, and an infant silence prevailed upon both men. I dared not move, the quiet was so striking.

At length, my friend spoke, "Quite so," he said softly, so that only the sudden stillness could account for his clarity. "We shall never best each other without besting ourselves, Mycroft."

"Well said, Sherlock," his brother replied. "It's lonely business, eh? At least we're still alive to appreciate each other. I'm off to the Diogenes. You're welcome, of course, though I doubt it to be your fare."

"I think not tonight," my companion replied.

"Of course," the other answered. "Then good night, Sherlock, and good luck in…er, best of fortune to you in the New Year!"

With that, Mycroft Holmes bade his driver on, and my friend returned the favour of his brother's tidings, unheard amidst the clamour of starting hooves.

As I slowly rose, Holmes remained slumped in the window frame. At length, he drew up the banner, regarding once the accumulated expanse of it in his hands, and then dropped it, in a pile, at his feet.

"Please forgive my treatment of you, old fellow," said Holmes. "I refer not only to the physical abuse, but my lack of attention to your natural curiosities regarding this affair. This pennant you see, is a thing of my past, a means of signaling across countryside taught me by my older brother."

"It has all become clear to me, Holmes," I offered, "true to your very words. Considering the perplexity of this challenge," here I tapped the cryptogram myself, "what other victory could possibly have been the reference? Also, upon reflection, I realize that the precise stroke of midnight is an irresistible target in such matters pertaining to allotted time. If I recall correctly, you observed that your brother managed delivery of the cypher upon the center stroke, the sixth of twelve, Christmas Eve."

"Precisely," said Holmes, with a relief which seemed to perceptively lift his spirits. Then, with a fusion of promise and dread, he added, "And we shall deal with Moriarty soon enough."

A veil of mystery lifted. My service revolver was put up and Holmes returned the crumpled flag, together with the abstruse cryptogram, to his private quarters.

"And what have we here?" Holmes asked on his return, having finally noticed the platter atop the side-board.

"Cold beef with cabbage and radish," I answered as my companion devoured a slice and offered the dish to me. "I've already eaten, Holmes. You were too engrossed to take notice," I declined.

"You've left substantially more than my share, my good fellow," he observed as he carried it to the dining table and set it down before him, "and I shall interpret that generosity as your wish."

"It is my professional advice, Holmes," I encouraged him to eat.

"Then I shall make every effort not to disappoint you," he replied between bites, adding, "I'm positively famished."

I could not refrain from regarding my friend, the famous detective, as he consumed the entire meal with such enthusiasm as to become an absolute entertainment. Holmes seemed to be similarly amused by the fervour with which he gorged himself, for he punctuated the entire process with outbursts of chortling, half- smothered by his feeding, which appeared to be beyond his suppression. I contributed a carafe of wine to this merriment, which my companion emptied as he finished off the last morsel of cabbage.

"And now I believe I shall sleep quite soundly," my friend proclaimed, rising wearily from the table, "for I am delirious with exhaustion."

"Of course."

"I shall be forever indebted to you," he offered, "for consideration of the service you provided me. Thank you, Watson. Good night."

As my friend turned to depart, I halted his exit saying simply "Sherlock?"

Unaccustomed as he was to my use of his given name, he stopped short, turned and replied, "Yes?"

"Your brother sought to wish you 'good luck' in the coming year. He corrected himself, knowing your contempt for the word. I was admonished on Christmas day for that very infraction."

"Your point being?"

"You must recall the moment when you first identified the cryptogram's symbols as being equations, and the circumstances that attended the moment – the *fortuitous* overlapping of the two puzzles."

"Of course, and you intend to charge me with having the benefit of some obscure concept of…

"Charge you!?", I interrupted, "Is being the recipient of good fortune, often referred to as *luck*, ever to be considered a transgression? Does it warrant accusation? Holmes! There's not a soul alive untouched by sheer luck in some fashion or other, some point in time or other!" At this juncture, I was carried away by my own audacity in confronting Holmes in this fashion on a point I knew to be a matter of pride. "I simply cannot grasp your aversion to the word. It's merely a word, Holmes! Why allow it to torment you with every utterance of it?!"

At this, Holmes regarded me with what appeared to be a sympathetic expression. He seemed to slump in capitulation and sheer weariness. I immediately regretted my outburst. But then, as I shuffled in place, glancing everywhere to avoid Holmes' eyes, he spoke.

"Watson…John, I had no idea that this issue was so significant to you. You are correct, of course, in citing 'luck' as merely a word. I question its origin. I'm suspicious of its existence. Whatever I cannot satisfactorily comprehend… distresses me. I know it was for my sake you broached the subject. The least I can do is return the favour. Yes, Watson, on that day, at that very moment of beholding the two cryptograms superimposed, I was…*lucky!*"

Holmes visibly winced as he spoke the word. But then, as if the single utterance of it had broken a spell, Holmes' stern expression softened. He smiled, and then began to chuckle, as quietly and privately as possible. Holmes' budding mirth was infectious, and soon both of us were sharing a merriment unknown since Christmas Eve.

As our cheer subsided, I sighed with relief, "Thank you, Holmes, and Happy New Year."

"Thank *you,* Watson, and Happy New Year."

With that, my friend withdrew from my company to afford himself a much-needed rest.

For my part, I discovered that, having napped most of the day, I was not at all weary. I'd not eaten since the single slice of beef, which now seemed a lifetime hence. Holmes had drained the wine, which I considered my last hope for achieving some measure of fatigue, and so, with something of an unwelcomed vigor, I resigned myself the task of setting pen to paper, accounting the adventures of my friend, Sherlock Holmes, whereupon it began to snow.

Epilogue

The Christmas week of 1889 remained a memorable one for Holmes and Watson throughout the balance of their years together. The bond of their friendship was strengthened during this time of mutual giving.

The exchange of a pen for a magnifying glass began the adventure of the Yuletide Puzzle, followed by acts of fondness and concern even as scrutiny of the cryptogram commanded the attention of both men.

Perhaps most meaningful is the sharing that Holmes bequeathed to Watson, revealing that the investigative exercises with which he confounds his companion are made with the knowledge and security that he "shall never be required to deduce anything more horrible than goodness". Clearly, this constitutes a profound gift both companions enjoyed throughout their relationship.

The puzzle itself is the manifestation of another gift, given in the spirit of a camaraderie born of familial love, and symbolized by a red flag.

About The Author

Ed Trotta is a fifty-year veteran of the Broadway stage, prime-time television, and feature film. He has portrayed Sherlock Holmes in two stage productions: "The Sign of Four" at the Roundhouse Theatre in Maryland, and in a world premiere stage adaptation of his original manuscript at the Summit Theatre in West Virginia. No stranger to iconic and legendary characters, Trotta has also performed as Dracula, The Man of La Mancha, Cyrano de Bergerac, MacBeth, and Abraham Lincoln.

A native New Yorker, Ed Trotta now lives in Los Angeles, where he has served as president of The Company of Angels, L.A.'s oldest repertory company. His stage adaptations include "A Clockwork Orange", "Animal Farm", "Moby Dick" and "Kafka's "The Trial". Ed is the recipient of 13 Dramalogue awards, 3 Ovation nominations (West Coast Tonys), and many Critics' Picks. Ed Trotta has written a one-man play, "Two Miles A Penny", in which he portrays Abraham Lincoln, and in which he has toured nationally.

Most notable among Ed Trotta's voice-over credits is the ongoing role of Malfurion Stormrage, a heroic character in the popular interactive game, "World of Warcraft".

"Sherlock Holmes in the Case of the Yuletide Puzzle" is Mr. Trotta's first novel.

MX Publishing

MX Publishing brings the best in new Sherlock Holmes novels, biographies, graphic novels and short story collections every month. With over 500 books it's the largest catalogue of new Sherlock Holmes books in the world.

We have over one hundred and fifty Holmes authors. The majority of our authors write new Holmes fiction - in all genres from very traditional pastiches through to modern novels, fantasy, crossover, children's books and humour.

In Holmes biography we have award winning historians including Alistair Duncan, Brian Pugh and Maureen Whittaker who have all won the Sherlock Holmes Book of The Year Award.

MX Publishing also has one of the largest communities of Holmes fans on Facebook and Twitter under @mxpublishing.

MX is a social enterprise that has raised over $100,000 for good causes including Happy Life Mission (Kenya), Undershaw School for children with learning disabilities (UK) and the WFP (World Food Programme).

www.mxpublishing.com

Also from MX Publishing

"Phil Growick's, 'The Secret Journal of Dr Watson', is an adventure which takes place in the latter part of Holmes and Watson's lives. They are entrusted by HM Government (although not officially) and the King no less to undertake a rescue mission to save the Romanovs, Russia's Royal family from a grisly end at the hand of the Bolsheviks. There is a wealth of detail in the story but not so much as would detract us from the enjoyment of the story. Espionage, counter-espionage, the ace of spies himself, double-agents, double-crossers...all these flit across the pages in a realistic and exciting way. All the characters are extremely well-drawn and Mr Growick, most importantly, does not falter with a very good ear for Holmesian dialogue indeed. Highly recommended. A five-star effort."
The Baker Street Society

www.mxpublishing.com

www.mxpublishing.com

Also from MX Publishing

The Detective and The Woman Series

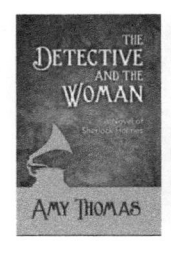

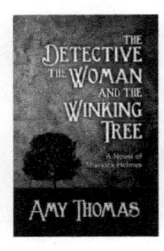

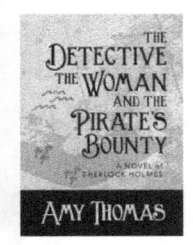

The Detective and The Woman

The Detective, The Woman and The Winking Tree

The Detective, The Woman and The Silent Hive

The Detective, The Woman and The Pirate's Bounty

"The book is entertaining, puzzling and a lot of fun. I believe the author has hit on the only type of long-term relationship possible for Sherlock Holmes and Irene Adler. The details of the narrative only add force to the romantic defects we expect in both of them and their growth and development are truly marvelous to watch. This is not a love story. Instead, it is a coming-of-age tale starring two of our favorite characters."

Philip K Jones

www.mxpublishing.com

Also from MX Publishing

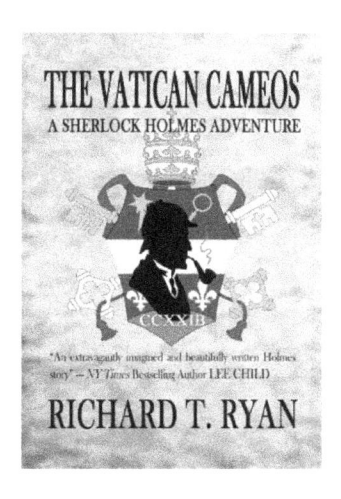

When the papal apartments are burgled in 1901, Sherlock Holmes is summoned to Rome by Pope Leo XII. After learning from the pontiff that several priceless cameos that could prove compromising to the church, and perhaps determine the future of the newly unified Italy, have been stolen, Holmes is asked to recover them. In a parallel story, Michelangelo, the toast of Rome in 1501 after the unveiling of his Pieta, is commissioned by Pope Alexander VI, the last of the Borgia pontiffs, with creating the cameos that will bedevil Holmes and the papacy four centuries later. For fans of Conan Doyle's immortal detective, the game is always afoot. However, the great detective has never encountered an adversary quite like the one with whom he crosses swords in "The Vatican Cameos.."

"An extravagantly imagined and beautifully written Holmes story"
(**Lee Child**, NY Times Bestselling author, Jack Reacher series)

Also from MX Publishing

The Conan Doyle Notes (The Hunt For Jack The Ripper)
"Holmesians have long speculated on the fact that the Ripper murders aren't mentioned in the canon, though the obvious reason is undoubtedly the correct one: even if Conan Doyle had suspected the killer's identity he'd never have considered mentioning it in the context of a fictional entertainment. Ms Madsen's novel equates his silence with that of the dog in the night-time, assuming that Conan Doyle did know who the Ripper was but chose not to say – which, of course, implies that good old stand-by, the government cover-up. It seems unlikely to me that the Ripper was anyone famous or distinguished, but fiction is not fact, and "The Conan Doyle Notes" is a gripping tale, with an intelligent, courageous and very likable protagonist in DD McGil."
The Sherlock Holmes Society of London

www.mxpublishing.com

Also from MX Publishing

The American Literati Series

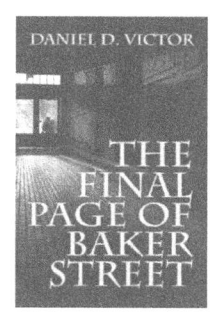

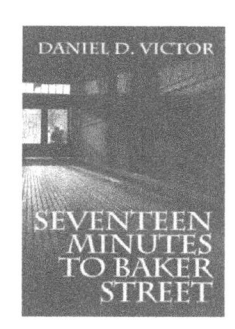

The Final Page of Baker Street
The Baron of Brede Place
Seventeen Minutes To Baker Street

"The really amazing thing about this book is the author's ability to call up the 'essence' of both the Baker Street 'digs' of Holmes and Watson as well as that of the 'mean streets' of Marlowe's Los Angeles. Although none of the action takes place in either place, Holmes and Watson share a sense of camaraderie and self-confidence in facing threats and problems that also pervades many of the later tales in the Canon. Following their conversations and banter is a return to Edwardian England and its certainties and hope for the future. This is definitely the world before The Great War."
Philip K Jones

www.mxpublishing.com

CPSIA information can be obtained
at www.ICGtesting.com
Printed in the USA
BVHW030031291022
650363BV00011B/913